FICTION FROM THE UK

Edited By Sarah Waterhouse

First published in Great Britain in 2024 by:

YoungWriters
Est. 1991

Young Writers
Remus House
Coltsfoot Drive
Peterborough
PE2 9BF
Telephone: 01733 890066
Website: www.youngwriters.co.uk

Printed and bound in the UK by BookPrintingUK
Website: www.bookprintinguk.com
YB0587AZ

FOREWORD

Welcome Reader!

Are you ready to discover weird and wonderful creatures that you'd never even dreamed of?

For Young Writers' latest competition we asked primary school pupils to create a creature of their own invention, and then write a story about it using just 100 words - a hard task! However, they rose to the challenge magnificently and the result is this fantastic collection full of creepy critters and bizarre beasts!

Here at Young Writers our aim is to encourage creativity in children and to inspire a love of the written word, so it's great to get such an amazing response, with some absolutely fantastic stories.

Not only have these young authors created imaginative and inventive creatures, they've also crafted wonderful tales to showcase their creations. These stories are brimming with inspiration and cover a wide range of themes and emotions - from fun to fear and back again!

I'd like to congratulate all the young authors in this anthology, I hope this inspires them to continue with their creative writing.

CONTENTS

Hafsah Khan (8)	59
Khansa Haroon (8)	60
Hafsa Salim (8)	61
Mohammed Rizwan (8)	62
Kirill Nesteruk (8)	63
Malikai Campbell (8)	64

Hampton Dene Primary School, Hampton Dene

Maya Sheehan (9)	65
Alexandros Raptis (10)	66
Mary Thomas (9)	67
Fin Cooter (9)	68

Oasis Academy Hobmoor, Yardley

Ammara Khan (7)	69
Salina Mahmood (10)	70
Aroush Kashif (9)	71
Zaynab Hussain (8)	72
Sanaya Jabeen Attiq (8)	73
Logan Callow (11)	74
Inaya Asif (8)	75
Aysal Hajati (9)	76

Queen Boudica Primary School, Colchester

Ciyanna Nyika (8)	77
Andrew Anish (9)	78
Sharen Gnanavel (8)	79
Umar Tufail (9)	80

Ralph Sadleir Middle School, Puckeridge

Lyla Taylor (10)	81
Freddie Durr (11)	82
Beau Tollfree (10)	83
Jodie Smith (11)	84
Ostyn Barron (10)	85
Levente Radics (10)	86
Amber York	87

| Zoe Barton (10) | 88 |
| Alfie Faber (10) | 89 |

St Joseph's Catholic Primary School, Langwith Junction

Joseph Hall (10)	90
Alan Michalik (10)	91
Adon Sijo (11)	92
Beatrix Fisher (10)	93
Elizabeth Batterbee (10)	94
Bunja Sanno (11)	95
Maja Wator (10)	96
Abibatou Kassama (10)	97
Briana Carmody (11)	98
Aoife Harper (10)	99
Lola Gale (10)	100
Freddie Marriott (10)	101
Zitel Onyeneke (10)	102

St Paul's Cathedral School, London

Alice Jamieson (9)	103
Emmeline Farrow (9)	104
Madeleine Hirst (8)	105
Victoria Elisa Adell Peric (9)	106
Ariana Mangal (8)	107
Daniel Snowden (9)	108
Jaxon Reilly Sweeney (9)	109
Jack Nelson (8)	110
Francesca Chopin (8)	111
Raphael Sen (9)	112
Minjun Kim (8)	113
Henry Kay (9)	114
Vivienne Roberts	115
Gustas Ciapas	116
Noah Middleton Targett (8)	117
Lyra Evers (8)	118
Benjamin Lester (8)	119
Oscar Lampo (9)	120
Elsa Hildreth (8)	121
Oliver Dudley (8)	122

The Ridge Academy, Cheltenham

Ilyas Ali (9)	123
Leland Hannis (10)	124
Henry Holden (9)	125
Dominic Davis (7)	126
Charlie Bennett (10)	127
Lenny Aves (9)	128
Wyatt Campbell (7)	129
Riley Parker (8)	130
Archie Vaughan (8)	131
Micah Dewberry (9)	132
Junior (8)	133
Rowan Winterford (9)	134

Wynyard CE Primary School, Wynyard

Maisie Portas (8)	135
Hazel Swinney (8)	136
Anna McCaul (8)	137
Harjan Toor (8)	138
Naia Sedley (9)	139
Arabelle Waller (8)	140
Jaxon Dea (8)	141
Miles Heward (9)	142
Rishabh Mitra (8)	143
Amelia Robertson (9)	144
Alexander O'Rourke (9)	145
Matthew Brown (9)	146
Poppy Lightowler (9)	147
Toby Guyatt (9)	148
Luca Caruana (9)	149
Ben Maudlin (8)	150

THE STORIES

The Trip To Earth

"Run!" shouted Barney to Bob as another asteroid hit Planet Noon. They jumped into the spaceship and made their descent to Planet Earth.

"Phew, that was close," said Bob.

"Yeah," agreed Barney.

They soon made it to Planet Earth.

"Wow," breathed Barney as their feet touched the ground. Bob was jumping up and down excitedly but he jumped too high and started floating away.

"*Bob!*" screamed Barney as he started floating away too.

"Quick, get to the water!" yelled Bob. They made it to the water as they knew they were amazing swimmers.

"Phew," said a voice...

Cora Black (10)

Bangor Central Integrated Primary School, Bangor

The Revenge

On Jupiter, there's a man called Reat. He drove to his house. Reat was *shocked*. Cheeseman covered his house in... *cheese!* "Time for revenge!" Reat said, so he went to Cheeseman's house and put it on fire and went home happily until he went inside his home, it was full of *cheese!*

Cheeseman said, "That's what you get!" so, Reat Man chased him and Reat finally caught Cheeseman, so Reat said, "Bye," and threw him to *Venus!*

Cheeseman said, "Aah!" Reat Man went home, cleaned his house, went to his couch, ate popcorn and drank Fanta. But then, he heard a sound...

Alicja Chrust (11)

Bangor Central Integrated Primary School, Bangor

The Escaped Creature

In a lab, a creature was created. A dreadful, hairy beast! *"I hate humans! They deserve to die!"* the monster yelled...

Later on, the monster destroyed the town!

"You'll never hurt us!" yelled a boy. The brave boy lit a pile of wood on fire! Then, a group of people pushed the monster into the fire.

"Aah! *I will get my revenge!"* screamed the monster as he burned. Eventually, everyone who defeated the monster was thanked. So, so many people think that if the monster came back, it would almost be as bad as a bomb strike upon the people!

Alesha McMullan (10)

Bangor Central Integrated Primary School, Bangor

3

Spoonie's Spoons

One day, on Kitchen Moon, it felt wrong, every monster felt sick. Spoonie's house was shaking. The monsters all realised that Knifey was coming. Knifey came and he stole Forkie's forks and Spoonie's spoons. Spoonie decided to hide away from everyone and hid in a cave. Knifey thought it was funny. Forkie and Knifey got in a fight. Forkie poisoned Knifey and Knifey died. All Knifey's servants gave Spoonie his spoons back and Forkie his forks back. Forkie and Spoonie made a cooking show together and Knifey's servants became Forkie and Spoonie's servants. They lived happily.

Katie Elliott (10)
Bangor Central Integrated Primary School, Bangor

Super Scary Simon Fights Big Battler Bob

One day, Super Scary Simon was scaring an unsuspecting school. While the school was evacuating, Big Battler Bob came in and stopped him and saved the day.

"Stop, Super Scary Simon!" said Bob staring at Simon

"No!" shouted Simon.

They argued for another five minutes while the school watched. All of a sudden, Simon said, "Let's finish this with a battle!" and Bob agreed. They started the battle and Simon hit Bob really hard, but Bob took revenge with a sucker punch to the stomach. Then, Simon disappeared and Bob couldn't find him...

Jason Jiao (10)
Bangor Central Integrated Primary School, Bangor

5

The Crazy Chrismas Cat

One day, in Asda, our Catykane was trying to steal candy canes but he was found by the police. Catykane started running really fast, but he crashed into the Christmas tree and disappeared. There was a bang and Catykane jumped out and shot into a policeman's face and knocked him down. The people started screaming and running everywhere. Catykane took this opportunity and sat on a shelf, looking like a toy to hide. The police ran out, looking for him and Catykane sneakily escaped out of the shop. The police could never find him. Catykane comes to steal candy canes every year.

Christopher Higginson (10)

Bangor Central Integrated Primary School, Bangor

The Cyclops Demon Vs The Cat People

Boom! A building was destroyed. The Cat People were trying to take over the world, but the Cyclops Demon came to help humanity. Suddenly, the Cyclops Demon shot his laser eyes and wiped out half of The Cat People!

"Fire up," said The Cat People's captain. They launched a nuke at the Cyclops Demon, but they missed him by an inch.

"That was our last nuke," said The Cat People's deputy.

"Goodbye, Cat People," and then the Cyclops Demon shot his laser eyes and The Cat People were vanquished. The Cyclops Demon had won!

Ryan Walsh (11)
Bangor Central Integrated Primary School, Bangor

7

My Crazy Creature

Once upon a time, there was a creature named Jon. He was a pro footballer. He played for Tottenham, he was a striker, scoring hattricks left, right and centre. But one day, something unexpected happened. He got jumped by Spider-Man and they fought for hours and hours and hours until Jon hit Spider-Man with a really, really strong punch and knocked Spider-Man out the window. Jon thought he was dead and Jon thought his life would go back to normal until one day Spider-Man went back for round two, and this time it was different. Spider-Man threw Jon out the window and Jon died.

Jonah Edmunds (10)
Bangor Central Integrated Primary School, Bangor

The First Day Of Crazy Creature School

Demon Duck was worried about going to a new school called Crazy Creature School. Demon Duck couldn't sleep all night, he thought he was going to get bullied.

The next day was the first day of his new school. He was scared but he got dressed anyway, went downstairs, had breakfast; his favourite, bacon and eggs.

Demon Duck's Mum drove him to school. When he got to school, he went to class. He was the only duck, so everyone stared at him, but there was a girl called Daisy Duck and her boyfriend, Donald Duck. They were bullying him, Demon Duck told on them.

Leah McAuley (11)

Bangor Central Integrated Primary School, Bangor

9

The Unbreakable Friendship

It was a warm day in Water World, perfect for going in the sea. Skyler loved Water World but wanted to go somewhere new.
A couple of days later, she left for the airport. When she arrived there, she was scared. She started walking towards the seats. When she tripped over, someone helped her up. She realised it was someone from Fire Land, but they went and sat together. They were going to the same place. After the journey, they became best friends and did everything together. They got a house in a town where everyone was welcome. They then lived happily ever after.

Bethany McAvoy (10)
Bangor Central Integrated Primary School, Bangor

Mission Failed

When I-ball was just a baby, it was sent down to Earth for a mission: to have Planet Earth all to themselves!
All grown up, I-ball was a master at finding. One day, I-ball was searching but no one was there! I-ball searched high and low but still nothing! I-ball eventually gave up. I-ball was very, very sad because this was the first time they couldn't find anybody! But suddenly, I-ball heard footsteps, they were very, very close. But when I-ball looked over, there were all the people I-ball had frozen! And as soon as I-ball looked over, it was now frozen!

Lexie Mulholland (10)
Bangor Central Integrated Primary School, Bangor

YoungWriters®

The Nightmare Bat

The stars twinkling, the moon shining bright but it's no ordinary night. It's a nightmare! As they teleport through wardrobes, when they arrive at house 102, the little ghost goes and distracts the little girl while Nightmare Bat puts the nightmare dust on the pillow. When the little ghost goes invisible and sprinkles some dust so the girl forgets and goes back to sleep, they finally arrive at the last house. They realise it's not any house, it's house 209! When they teleport into the wardrobe, they see the kid up with a net! Will they get caught?!

Emma Armour (9)
Bangor Central Integrated Primary School, Bangor

Friendly Family

Friendy was born in Space. Her mother's name is Monster Anna. Her father's name is Crazy Fredy. Her brother's name is Kindly. Her family is so kind. Her family has four members. She has lots of friends, no enemies. Her brother was born in Monster Town. Her brother scared other creatures. She is six years old. Her brother is ten years old. Her mother is a good cook. Her father is leader of Monster Club.

But she and her brother don't like to live in space, they like to live in Monster Town. But her father and mother like to live in space.

Janani Rajesh (11)
Bangor Central Integrated Primary School, Bangor

13

Deep In The Forest

A lumberjack in Helldeath Forest hears thuds. Next second, he gets lifted up. *It* screeches, Tom stabs it. The monster yells and drops Tom, the army arrives, shoots at the monster. The monster kicks and they fall and die. The monster nips the lumberjack's arms, legs, then head.

Researcher: The guardian of the forest is peaceful, although when *it* feels under threat it won't stop till you die. He has killed people in real life and if you hear his screams or see him, it's too late for your life and you will die painfully.

Corey Wilson (11)

Bangor Central Integrated Primary School, Bangor

Pluto The Dwarf Planet

One day, in the year 4023, Andy was playing on his Xbox 500,000 with Claud from Glasgow, and he started teasing Andy because he lived on Pluto and humans were planning on going to Pluto to find new resources. Andy didn't believe this until the next day when Andy was watching Pickleball with Ally Alien and Tina, and their team was about to win when, suddenly, Andy's mum burst into the living room and told Tina and Ally that they had to go home. When Andy asked why, his mum said that the humans were coming. Andy was moving to Saturn's Rings.

Lydia McCoy (10)
Bangor Central Integrated Primary School, Bangor

Eva Star And The Evil Babysitter!

It was a normal day in Eva's home until her babysitter started yelling at Eva's little sister, Jess, to clean everywhere in the house. Eva had enough, she turned around, looking hideous and shot lighting out of her hands and the babysitter flew around the room! There was chaos!

An hour later, her mum came back to the house... it was *destroyed!* And the babysitter was *gone!* She took everything in the house. Eva ran out to find the babysitter, she shot lighting at the babysitter and she fell to the ground. Eva was a hero!

Emily Mullan (11)
Bangor Central Integrated Primary School, Bangor

The Bad Dave Trump

Dave Trump was playing Xbox. He was playing a really hard game, then he lost in the game and he threw his controller at the TV. *Boom!* His TV went up in flames. Dave ran out his house and called 999. But his call didn't get through, so he rushed outside and got all the neighbours out of their houses. So he could do his master plan. He was going to blow them up. Three, two, one... it failed. The neighbours ran away scared and called the police.

Ten seconds later, the police arrived. Dave was sent to jail for the rest of his days.

Finlay Mcrae (10)
Bangor Central Integrated Primary School, Bangor

A Day In The Life Of Krystallaria

Krystallaria leapt above rocks and roamed free in the jungles of Gloatus until she heard a rattle coming from the bushes! A human quickly came out! They turned around with shock as Krystallaria flew away! They yelled after her, but it was no use. She was shocked to the bone. She landed in a place far off, but wolves found her! She fought them until she heard a growl. A bear charged into them and they all ran. Krystallaria stopped and hypnotised the bear. She made it sleep. The wolves thanked her and left her alone. And this was *one* day.

Farah Peacock (11)
Bangor Central Integrated Primary School, Bangor

Seanna And The Portals!

One day, Seanna was swimming in the dark and misty ocean and met a nice mermaid called Pearl. They were exploring the large waters when they found a portal and they went through it, they ended up on a mysterious beach! When they got there, they saw that Pearl had feet and not a tail! And then saw it! They saw the *sand monster!* They fought as hard as they could, throwing water and pearls at him, then they defeated him! After they defeated him, they saw something in the distance. It was another portal! They stepped through the portal...!

Laura Fitzsimons (10)
Bangor Central Integrated Primary School, Bangor

19

The Attack Of The Monster

One day, there was a monster called Claud. Claud lived in Glasgow. It was a normal day until the monster attacked. The city was being destroyed, people were running to try and get away until the monster cornered them. Claud realised this and he jumped in and tried to distract the monster. The monster then went for Claud, but then Claud called for a friend and his friend was the Loch Ness Monster. The Loch Ness Monster scared the monster away and Claud thanked him, and he went back in the river and the entire city was saved and Claud was happy.

Charlie Campbell (10)
Bangor Central Integrated Primary School, Bangor

Crazy Bob And The Crazy Day

Crazy Bob has crazy hair and is very fast. He has a dog called Crazy Bob Jr. They hate people, so they stole some kids with their sweets and hid them in an apartment. Crazy Bob Jr fights off the people. Crazy Bob gets very angry because he doesn't get free sweets from the Spar. The kids jumped out of the apartment with parachutes because it was on fire! After, Crazy Bob Jr jumped out with a parachute.

Crazy Bob is still running with the sweets. Then, the police arrest Crazy Bob and Jr. So, they have to stay in prison for life.

Archie Millar (10)

Bangor Central Integrated Primary School, Bangor

Rusty Spoon Man

It is a dark morning in the classroom and Rusty Spoon Man is waiting outside a children's school in the rain, waiting for children.

The bell goes and all of the children come running out of the school. One tasty and scrumptious-looking child comes out of school and Rusty Spoon Man pulls him underground into his base that can't be seen from the top. Then, Rusty Spoon Man steals everyone's rusty spoons and now he has thousands of rusty spoons. He is now happy because his life achievement is to have all the rusty spoons.

Toby Lack (11)
Bangor Central Integrated Primary School, Bangor

Craball

It was a dark and dingy night and there was a crazy creature called Ballgie. When he was scared, he would turn into a big bouncy bowling ball. There is a big scary dragon called Dragoon and he bullied Ballgie and called him names like Bally McFally. However, Ballgie just ignored him and got on with life. He went to a big, scary park. There were lots of kids and parents at the big, scary park. Ballgie bounced back to his little house and went to sleep! Ballgie had lots of nightmares that night and cried himself to sleep!

Brody Brown (11)
Bangor Central Integrated Primary School, Bangor

YoungWriters
Est. 1991

The Hill

One day, in the year 4023, Tina decided to go and visit Andy the alien, but what she didn't know was there was a huge hill blocking the way! She was bewildered, she tried flying over it but it was too tall, she tried and tried until it turned dark at sunset. Tina tried everything, but nothing worked. She eventually tried to go round it, but it was too wide. She was going to miss Pickleball! She didn't want to let Andy down, so she flew with all her might and made it! But when she got there, he said he was moving...

Faith Jackson (10)
Bangor Central Integrated Primary School, Bangor

Drama On Sock Soul Planet

Do you ever notice that a pair of your socks are missing? Well, that was Sam. It was one morning on Sock Soul Planet when Sam heard that all his socks were going to be taken by his biggest enemy, the washing machine. So, Sam the Smelly Sock Sneaker/Stealer decided to build a shelter to put all his socks into. So, Sam did that and then the washing machine came dramatically to Sock Soul Planet. But what happened was the washing machine took Sam instead, but nobody knew the ending. So, this smelly story is to be continued...

Lexie Cree (10)
Bangor Central Integrated Primary School, Bangor

YoungWriters® Est. 1991

Wig Snatcher

It was a dull day on the beach. Wig Snatcher felt unhappy, he had no hair and no wigs and he thought he should have a wig. So, he started looking into shops, trying to find a wig. When all hope was lost, he found someone with a wig. He swung his hand and snatched it off his head and he finally had a wig, and every day he would go out snatching wigs until he snatched someone's real hair. He couldn't get his hand off. He panicked and, at that moment, everybody stole their wigs back and he was hairless once again.

Sophie Wilkes (11)
Bangor Central Integrated Primary School, Bangor

War Of The Flies

Rnzig is a one-eyed demon who was born in a rotten tomato in a kitchen. When he was in the kitchen, he spotted his worst enemy, a fly! He looked directly at it, which should have turned it inside out. But *he* turned inside out! So, he ran to his home (a rotten tomato). The fly ordered his other flies to attack! But half of the fly rebellion was drawn to the lights and killed! The rest of the army went buzzing furiously towards the tomato and started eating it! And that's the reason flies eat rotten food.

Yash J Hallsworth (10)
Bangor Central Integrated Primary School, Bangor

YoungWriters®
Est. 1991

Stolen Star

Sunny was living her life and enjoying it until, one day, Fire came from Fireland. She planned to steal the Happiness Star. When she stole it, a really loud alarm went off. Sunny heard, got her friends and fought to get the star back. Once she got it, she and her friends must try to send her out of Happy Village.

They worked together and sent her back to Fireland. They now have to return the star to the protector.

They have returned it and now can continue having fun and enjoying life in Happy Village.

Molly-Rose Bradley (10)
Bangor Central Integrated Primary School, Bangor

The Nightmare Blackout

One day, a girl named Elanore was having headaches. Strange headaches they were. They gave her a sense of fear and she felt empty inside. On an unusual day, she blacked out. She woke up but in what looked like space but darker. No stars at all!

She realised she had to get out. Suddenly, a dark shadow crept over her. It was the Nightmare. She had only heard about it in stories. She ran, running fast. It was sucking her into what looked like her nightmares. She closed her eyes and wished she was home...

Mollie Porter (11)

Bangor Central Integrated Primary School, Bangor

Ally The Unlucky Alien

Ally the alien was a very lucky alien (not for long) because he had been the alien that had been picked to travel to Earth to spy on the humans and see what they were up to. So, he got in his Spacepod and headed to Earth. Ally the alien was eleven in Earth years, so he had to go to school. But then, he realised something horrible. He had forgotten his disguise! On top of that, the energy in his Spacepod ran out when he landed on Earth! He had no way to travel back home and no way to tell his friends.

Lochlainn Canning (11)
Bangor Central Integrated Primary School, Bangor

The End Of The World

Long ago, there was a statue that came to life. The creature's name was Ben. The creature wanted to destroy the world. He went to New York City so he could start there, But he had an enemy, a demon dog who also wanted to conquer the world. They fought long and hard, but in the end, Ben won. Then, he went on a journey. He went to many different places and learnt different things, tried different stuff and ate different foods. But when he found an enemy, he destroyed them and conquered everything.

Lucas Maxwell (11)
Bangor Central Integrated Primary School, Bangor

Destroyer

Darcee was living her life until her enemy Icey arrived at her planet, Greenland! Darcee pressed the emergency button, an alarm rang and her city heard it, but the whole planet didn't, so she called all of the kings and queens to tell them to ring their alarms. Soon, Darcee and Icey fought, half of the planet was now ice. Soon, Darcee made a deal with Icey, the deal was that Icey could have half of the planet and Darcee could have half. Icey agreed to the deal and there was no more war.

Georgia McConnell (10)

Bangor Central Integrated Primary School, Bangor

The End Of Time

The Planet Destroyer used to be a little monster, but he got turned into a bad one after he got stuck in a machine, then turned into a terrible monster. But when he destroyed his first world, he felt bad for them, so he made a new world called Earth, brainwashed all their minds and destroyed 5,000 years of their work and no one knew. But he was defeated by his own son and he said to his son to carry on his work and fix all the bad things he did. He died but he will never be forgotten.

Arif Shah (10)
Bangor Central Integrated Primary School, Bangor

The Escape

On Planet Citron, Spbob was relaxing and having a nap and then he heard the sirens go off because Planet Citron was about to explode. So, he sprinted as fast as he could and made it to the escape pods. He got to Earth just in time and then he landed on Earth. Now he is very angry, so he destroyed everything in his way. He is angrier than the Hulk from Marvel.

Anyway, back to the story. He got so angry, exploded the whole universe. Now there is a boy finding his body parts...

Reece Murphy (10)
Bangor Central Integrated Primary School, Bangor

The Big Heist

CatNap was a cat that lived in Paris, that could use her tongue to strangle people with her enemy, DogDay. They both wanted the Mona Lisa. But one day, CatNap decided to try and steal the Mona Lisa. Suddenly, out of nowhere, DogDay appeared to also steal the Mona Lisa! They both had a big fight. CatNap used her really long tongue to strangle DogDay! Sadly, DogDay died. CatNap stole the Mona Lisa and CatNap lived in Paris and kept on stealing with her new enemy, SnakeTake.

Freddie Moore (11)
Bangor Central Integrated Primary School, Bangor

Elemental Devil Vs Elemental God

My story is about a war between Elemental God and Elemental Devil (my character is Elemental Devil). Basically, Elemental God started the war. The first attack of Elemental Devil's was his elemental sabre earth attack. In one attack, Elemental God died. But Elemental God was acting, and suddenly Elemental God attacked with his air sabre. In one hit, Elemental Devil flew to the sky. What happened next? Is Elemental Devil alive? Can Elemental Devil fight back again?

Safwan Wadi (11)
Bangor Central Integrated Primary School, Bangor

The Godtree

The Godtree was in the woods and was eating humans and stealing their energy, but a man came to battle the Godtree. The man and his brother battled the beast. It tried to put them into a dream world, but they defeated it. They shone their power and he got sealed into himself. But the Godtree used its power to mock the man and son's battle so it could revive, back to the world of the living. It was separated into ten creatures, but it was coming back...

Jehangir Mahmood (11)
Bangor Central Integrated Primary School, Bangor

37

Dry Land

It was a normal day at alien school in class 2A when Tech Robot got an alert on his screen that Water Wart was sucking up all the water on the planet. The Tech Robot said he was going to get some fresh air, so he went outside to go and fight Water Wart. He activated his guns and jetpack and flew into the sky and started firing missiles at Water Wart and knocked Water Wart down, and then wrapped him up and gave him to the police.

Adam Seeds (10)
Bangor Central Integrated Primary School, Bangor

The Final Stand

Ragnor is in his kingdom of Saudi Arabia. The Americans attack his kingdom. They blow up one of Ragnar's castles because he is the son of an evil god. Rangnor gathered all of his troops to go and attack, they marched to America to destroy and blow everything up. Ragnar escaped, going from country to country, destroying them all. He became king of the world, but suddenly, another god appeared to try and destroy him...

Jack Connolly (10)
Bangor Central Integrated Primary School, Bangor

Stick Man

It was the morning after Christmas when Stick Man went for a run in the park, when a dog spotted him. He knew that the dog was faster than him. He got caught by the dog. Stick Man travelled so far. First, the dog dropped him off into a river, then a beach, then a forest, then a frozen forest. He thought he saw the family tree, but no. What was that in the distance? Santa! He kept waving his hands at the sleigh...

Teddy Mcilwaine (11)
Bangor Central Integrated Primary School, Bangor

The Great Escape

It has been three months, one week and five days since I was thrown in prison. King Rooz is so evil, I must get out of here!
At lunch, the guards went by, I dug a hole. I saw something in the distance. It was a giant standing behind King Rooz. I saw the guards. I ran faster and faster, but I fell down a hole. In the far distance, I heard 'Welcome to the end', yet I was free.

Aran Thompson (10)
Bangor Central Integrated Primary School, Bangor

Ballan's Revenge

"Noooo!" Ballan shouted as he saw his lifelong friend being kicked over a fence as he was supposed to go into the net.

That started his revenge.

"I will cut and saw *every* net I see!" He and his father developed saws as hands and an antenna for speaking. Then, he started his journey to cut and saw every football net.

Caleb Banke (11)
Bangor Central Integrated Primary School, Bangor

Develishaurus!

As the slimy worms wriggled around urgently, Devilshaurus lay on his bed (which was very dirty), thinking about what he should do. Suddenly, an amazing idea popped up in his head.

He flew around the polluted air when he found his victim. A small, childish girl was sitting in her room, she covered her face in sadness after hearing the monster's disheartening words from above. Develishaurus smirked as he left her room. Suddenly, he catapulted down onto the grass below. Devilishaurus angrily looked up, when he saw Kindotaur looking at his bright red eyes. Kindotaur quickly pushed Devilishaurus backwards into the dark abyss...

Abiha Chughtai (11)
Caldmore Primary Academy, Walsall

Hairy Scary Monster Ball

Hairy Scary Monster Ball is really scary, but on the other hand, he is *verrrrry* shy. Before you read on, I'm going to tell you a little secret. But can you keep a secret? If you can, read on.
When he is shy, he turns into a red ball and hides his fur and looks like a regular red ball (even though he isn't).

Klaudia Kaczmarczyk (11)
Campsmount Academy, Norton

The Boogey Man

The Boogey Man feeds off of fear.
Say his name in the mirror three times at 3:33 in the morning, he will come out and kill you.
His hand is a sharp crowbar.

Carlton Mannion (12)
Campsmount Academy, Norton

The Crazy Monster Theme Park

One day, there was a monster called Glum, he was always sad. But one day, Glum met another girl monster who had green eyes and bumpy purple skin. Her name was Sally.

Sally said, "Oh, hello there, what's your name?"

"Me? Oh, I'm Glum," he said. Sally asked him to go to the crazy monster theme park. "Sure, why not? But I'm scared of heights," said Glum.

"Oh, that's okay, let's go on the highest roller coaster in the whole entire world!" Sally dragged him to the highest roller coaster in the world. He had the best time of his life, Glum said quietly.

Ayva Harte (8)
George Betts Primary Academy, Smethwick

The Monster Who Lost His Arm

Once upon a time, there was a creature, a scary creature. A bad guy threw a knife at him, so the creature lost his arm.

Immediately, a guy called Michal rushed to him and helped him before the monster died. The monster was greedy, but when Michal healed the monster, he became kind. Michal created a family with the monster.

Michal forgot that the next day was his birthday, so he took the monster to his house and had fun. But there was a problem, the monster had a family. However, the monster's family also wanted to live with Michal.

They all became a family in Michal's house.

Denis Marin (9)

George Betts Primary Academy, Smethwick

47

The Dragon That Breathed Hot Sauce

Once, there was a dragon named Alfie. Every other dragon breathed fire except for him. He breathed hot sauce and that was why other dragons were afraid of him. One day, everything changed after a girl named Nina met him.

Alfie was flying around his land, feeling glum. Suddenly, a girl named Nina stopped him from flying. Alfie was confused but listened. Nina said that she could change his life. She was a wizard and could change his breathing to fire. She pointed her stick to him and changed his breathing to fire. All the dragons played with him after knowing.

Arina Everest (8)

George Betts Primary Academy, Smethwick

Fire And Ice Dragons

One day, an ice dragon went to get food. He saw a fire dragon. Ice Dragon got scared, he went to his mom, he got very scared. He told his mom that he saw a fire dragon. His mom said, "Don't go there, they can eat you."

One day, a fire dragon stole the ice dragons' food. Now they've got less food for winter. They were so nervous.

One day, the ice dragon went to the fire dragon and said, "Please leave us alone," and the fire dragon was trying to eat him, but the ice dragon was fast. Finally, the fire dragon didn't eat him.

Miqdad Saif (9)

George Betts Primary Academy, Smethwick

The Monstrous Villain

This creepy monster is an eating-blood-only machine. This terrifying creature, when he sees a person, he will eat their soul. He's not only powerful, he is special. He can turn invisible and tiny. One day, he was only a natural kid, but his dad was a villain and turned him into a robotic villain. His name is Blood Demon and Soul Stealer because he steals 4,000 souls every day. Also, he owns fifty lands because he took them over with a hook and the people were gone. He will die if they hit 2,000 bombs, but he has another robotic person, his brother...

Abu-Bakr Raza (8)
George Betts Primary Academy, Smethwick

The Fire Dragon

Once upon a time, there was a boy called Eesa. He was a dragon collector. He had caught every Elemental dragon. But he longed to collect the rarest one, the fire dragon, with its dirty-blonde eyes, scarlet scales and razor-sharp prickles out the end of his back. It was easily the hardest to collect out of all.

One day, he was walking, he saw a fire dragon. He ran home, got his net and bloodsucking ticks to lure the dragon. Finally, he ran and caught it. "Yes!" he screamed. He'd done it, finally his collection was complete!

Amelia Hussain (8)

George Betts Primary Academy, Smethwick

The Girl And The Monster

One day, there was a girl called Lilly, she loved the seaside. She would always go there and read a book, but one time she felt like going in a boat to the sea.

The next day, she did just that. She went and she saw animals like starfish, fish and others. But then, one day, she saw something in the distance. "Aah, aah, monster!" she shouted. The monster came closer and closer until he got to her.

He said, "Hi, my name is Jolly," in a terrifying voice, then he did something really, really terrifying...

Harman Kaur (9)
George Betts Primary Academy, Smethwick

The Monster Land

Once, there was a monster land. There were monsters in that land. There were humans, the monsters wanted to take over their land and make the humans slaves.

There was a boy named Ethan, and his family didn't want them to be slaves. They were really poor. every day they had to be slaves or the monsters would eat them.

One day, a boy named Danny wanted to kill the monsters because they ate his whole family. He became a soldier and trained hard to battle, then he came to the monster land and defeated all the monsters.

Fathimah Younis (9)
George Betts Primary Academy, Smethwick

The Crash!

Once upon a time, there lived a girl called Lanely. She lived in a city, New York. And she lived by herself. She always feels lonely every day. But then, one night, there was a UFO flying around the neighbourhood. The UFO crashed on Lanely's house. Something was in it, it was a creature, the creature knocked on the door, so Lanely opened the door. She was shocked at what she saw...! She saw a strange creature, so she slammed the door and shut the blinds. It was an alien. The alien was confused at why she slammed the door...

Sabeeha Ali (9)
George Betts Primary Academy, Smethwick

The Story Of The Biggest Monster

There once was a hydra, which was the biggest monster out of every monster. It had sharp teeth and long legs to peek at the monsters. Its powers were like a toxic fog and he was the terrifying question. His other powers were like a noxious shot. Then he met a little monster which was a cyclops, and he scared it and it was frightened. It ran away and the hydra chased him a long way and went on another island. He got confused, so he looked around the place. Out of nowhere, a horde of monsters rushed at him and he was defeated.

Daryan Hamad (8)
George Betts Primary Academy, Smethwick

The Girl Who Never Gave Up

Once, there was a girl called Sydney and when she was four, she was afraid of monsters and when she went to sleep, she slept next to her mom. Sydney cried every night for her mom when she was not next to her.

Now she is eight and one night a giant monster, Rascal, came and destroyed the city. She was brave to fight Rascal. She had to fight for weeks! After four weeks, she stopped and gave up. After, Sydney had a plan. She gave a watermelon to Rascal. While Rascal was eating, she finally got him. She never gave up.

Amna Shahzad (7)
George Betts Primary Academy, Smethwick

The Scary Monster

Once upon a time, there was a scary monster called Chunky. He was so scary, everybody respected him so they did not get eaten. His friend is a ghost that used to live in a cool house. Once, he heard a terrifying noise. He got scared, so he left and took his clothes and his belongings. Little did he know somebody was following him.

The next day, he suddenly disappeared, so Chunky went to his friend's house but he did not know his friend was gone. He was in a stranger's house and he turned into a creepy ghost...

Alisha Fatima (9)
George Betts Primary Academy, Smethwick

Creature Of Fire

Once, there was an ant and it was scared because of a creature that blows fire out of himself. The creature was coming up to him and he knew he was a creature that kills ants. The ant got scared, so he ran away and when he was running away, he ran out of breath. He stopped, but the creature was gone and the ant was so happy because the creature was gone.

Then, the ant was going home to his family and when he got in and looked out the window, he saw the creature, so he quickly ducked his head down...

Lexie Beecroft (8)
George Betts Primary Academy, Smethwick

The Cool Snake And Wolf

Once upon a time, there was a snake and a wolf that came out of nowhere. When the children were learning, the wolf came up to this one child because she smelled like meat. The snake was going to eat her, but this kid came out of nowhere and grabbed the snake on the back. The wolf got very angry and had the courage to eat the little boy, but the boy threw meat. The wolf and snake jumped to the meat as fast as they could, but the boy had nothing to eat. The girl shared her food with the boy.

Hafsah Khan (8)
George Betts Primary Academy, Smethwick

The Monster Ate The Humans

Once upon a time, there was a monster called Narnia. He was not kind at all. He came back to humans and gobbled them up. He went to this island, only one person was left. She knew she had to get the stone. The portal was high up in the sky, so she tried to jump, finally reached the leg of the monster and raced with the monster. She reached it, the suction. If she stayed, then she would die. She rushed to the world. She would close the portal and eventually have to give everyone a potion...

Khansa Haroon (8)
George Betts Primary Academy, Smethwick

Kate And The Monster

Once, there was a girl called Lilly. One day, when she was getting ready for school, she was telling her mom that there was going to be a new kid in her class.

When she reached school, the new person was a boy, it was a monster. She was scared of the monster, but she had to try to talk to him, so she said hi to the creature. His name was Sam. When the girl went home, she told her mom all about it. Her mom said he could be kind, so she went to his house and they became good friends.

Hafsa Salim (8)
George Betts Primary Academy, Smethwick

The Lost Creature

Once upon a time, a monster went to sea and he found a boat. He went on it and it went so fast, he got to the middle of the sea. He had the power to make it take him to a shipwreck which had the powers to make monsters his friends.
The monster had three horns, two long arms and a power called Sprint Away. Sprinty was the creature's name. Before long, the monster was in his boat and he used his power. He saw an island which was a few centimetres from them. He was not lost!

Mohammed Rizwan (8)
George Betts Primary Academy, Smethwick

A Girl Who Got Scared About Monsters

One day, there was a girl who was named Casd. She liked a monster, so she played with it and after, it was night and the monster was under her bed. The monster has sharp teeth and slime on his back and the monster has arms that are sharp. The monster was ready to jump-scare her, but Casd looked around and didn't see anything and she fell asleep. The monster was back under the bed and Casd was thirsty, so she drank the cup and she went back to bed and the monster did.

Kirill Nesteruk (8)
George Betts Primary Academy, Smethwick

The Dragon That Wanted To Destroy The City

A dragon was destroying the city, but a boy called Migdad would save the city.

He hit the dragon, then the dragon got hurt. The dragon breathed fire on him. The boy dodged it, then the dragon breathed fire again and again until Migdad was tired of trying to get him. He started to slow down to have a break, then the dragon said, "It is time to die." Migdad had a shield to not let him die, then he cut him with the sword, then the dragon died in peace.

Malikai Campbell (8)
George Betts Primary Academy, Smethwick

The Monster In Spottystream Land

In the magical land of Spottystream resided a young lad known as Double Trouble Terry. One fine day, as Terry strolled through the enchanting forest towards the school, he noticed a quiver in the foliage. Suddenly, a mysterious figure bolted out and sprinted towards Terry. Overwhelmed with fear, Terry shrieked, swiftly turned and rushed back towards the safety of his home. The hideous figure cackled before retreating into the undergrowth, awaiting its next victim.

Upon reaching home, Terry was trembling with fright. However, in the kitchen, his mother delightedly baked delectable cookies. Terry settled himself and recounted the chilling tale.

Maya Sheehan (9)

Hampton Dene Primary School, Hampton Dene

The Peeking Blinder

It was a rainy evening, but still enjoyable from the warmth of a home. The muffled pattering of rain was all Grey could hear from inside the safety of his bed - something moved: he knew it, he *saw* it. He wasn't in the slightest sure what it *was*, but it was something, and that concerned him enough to go to the safety of his mum, or so he thought, for little Grey never even left the confines of his room - let alone get to the hallway - this was *The One*'s doing. It was a horrible, inexorable event that would shake any of its victims to the core...

Alexandros Raptis (10)
Hampton Dene Primary School, Hampton Dene

Rose The Monster

Mist rose from the night's floor and filled the air. In the small town of Rosavil, the wind howling through the swaying trees, the twinkling stars flashing before *her* eyes, a glow came from the kitchen. Rosa went to investigate, there was a creature glowing as bright as the North Star. Staring at the creature whose name was Rose - her mission was: make everyone who was grumpy happy, forever. She grabbed Rosa and twirled her round and threw her on the sofa and started to do the Monster Mash... She jiggled and wiggled until Rosa was smiling from ear to ear.

Mary Thomas (9)
Hampton Dene Primary School, Hampton Dene

Jamal And The Wobblygong

One day, people observed a colossal, red, moving being coming at rapid haste, so everybody had to evacuate but only via spaceship. There was one boy who knew an additional way to escape. His name was Jamal. So, he told everybody his idea. First, he got his enormous microphone and yelled it out to half the planet. Then to another quarter of the planet and eventually to the rest of the world. The strategy was to get in the Wobblygong, then out to a harmless planet and make a home. The new planet was perfectly safe to live on.

Fin Cooter (9)
Hampton Dene Primary School, Hampton Dene

Monster Island

On a small and minuscule island no one had ever visited, millions and millions of different monsters lived there together in harmony. Some of these creatures were big, some were small, some were pink, some were blue and some were even rainbow.

One snowy day, when the monsters went out to play together, something unusual happened.

Crash! A new type of monster had appeared. They had two legs, two arms and a long body.

The new type of creatures were called humans. The monsters lived happily together, like before, and the humans promised to protect all the monsters no matter what.

Ammara Khan (7)
Oasis Academy Hobmoor, Yardley

The Holders Of Multiverses

On a snowy night, a snow-drenched flower gazed at me. My eyes glowed from the moonlight, creating sparkles. Desperate to pick it, I walked to the flower and picked it, the flower disappeared with a touch of my skin. My clothes changed into a beautiful snow glow dress with sparkling diamond lights. The snow gets absorbed into my dress and some strange path leads me to a table sitting in the middle of the beach. I came across a snow-shaped crystal that was glowing, it compelled me to pick it up, and inside was a black miniature notebook full of magical spells, I knew then it was destined for me.

Salina Mahmood (10)

Oasis Academy Hobmoor, Yardley

Crazy Creature

I was sitting in a mysterious park that I'd never seen before when, suddenly, the bushes rustled. I was confused but scared at the same time. My instincts led me to go to the bush. I slowly crept when something just popped out and terrified me! It was a... *dinosaur*. It growled at me, looking for food. I ran to the closest lake and grabbed a few small fish. I knew this wouldn't do, but at least it could eat. It had a marble back that was baby blue and midnight black. It started to come to me for pets then...

Aroush Kashif (9)
Oasis Academy Hobmoor, Yardley

The Sleepover

I was about to sleep in my bed when my mum kissed me goodnight. Then suddenly, I saw a red flash under my bed. I went to my mum and dad's bedroom and told Mum that there was a monster under my bed. Then, my mum led me back to my bedroom and she told me that there is no such thing as monsters.

So, tomorrow, I asked one of my friends if they could come to my house for a sleepover and she said, "Yeah, sure."

We saw the monster and took him home.

Zaynab Hussain (8)
Oasis Academy Hobmoor, Yardley

Interesting Gem

On a sunny summer morning, deep under the sea, was an interesting little gem. The gem was stared at by four sea creatures. Two mermaids and two fish. They all stared at it and then mermaid one said, "Whose interesting gem is this?"
Then, mermaid two said, "Let's investigate it."
Number one fish said, "Okay, let's bring it to the underground laboratory." Number two fish agreed. Then, they swam to the laboratory...

Sanaya Jabeen Attiq (8)
Oasis Academy Hobmoor, Yardley

The Nightmare Of Terror

Today, I was sleeping and then I dreamed of a tall, black figure peeking their eyes on me through my door. I gasped to wake up from this nightmare. I saw dozens of eyes in the dark. I rushed to turn on the lamp, I ran. When the eyes were gone, I'd woken up and it was morning. I went downstairs to eat, something was there as I was going to eat my sandwich...

Logan Callow (11)
Oasis Academy Hobmoor, Yardley

Crazy Facts

Fab Butterfly likes to stay in your teachers' food, he has false teeth.

Next, we have Snot Face, she loves to eat bogeys.

Then, we have Hairy Scary Baby. His most embarrassing moment ever is when his mom gave him pigtails.

Finally, we have the Destroyer and his favourite thing to do is shape-shift in the shadows, and he eats your homework.

Inaya Asif (8)
Oasis Academy Hobmoor, Yardley

A Mother Call

A daughter was in her room upstairs, doing her homework when, suddenly, she heard her mom call her to come downstairs to eat dinner. She jumped onto her feet and began making her way towards the stairs, but before she even took a step, hands grabbed her and pulled her into the laundry room beside the staircase...

Aysal Hajati (9)
Oasis Academy Hobmoor, Yardley

Love Yourself

Every day, Destiny compared herself to the popular kids in her school. She would always wish she was like them. One morning, Destiny was taking a stroll to the park when *boom!* A weird creature appeared in front of her. "W-what are you? W-where are you from?" she stuttered.

"I am Tranner and the second question isn't important. My enemy, Slimly, is controlling your brain," replied the creature.

"My brain?!" screeched Destiny.

"Yes, but remember, you must love yourself," Tranner said before disappearing.

From that day on, Destiny remembered the words uttered by the strange creature and remembered to always love herself.

Ciyanna Nyika (8)
Queen Boudica Primary School, Colchester

Creature Day

Boiling with rage, Theodore, the half spider half squirrel stood in front of Creature Academy. Where were his parents? Especially considering that it was such an important day. *Splash!* Suddenly, a car came hurtling around the corner, spraying water onto his uniform. That's when he saw his mum's wild grin laughing at his disgust. Displeased, he stepped inside where he saw someone sleeping in his seat. It was Theodore's father! It is interesting how that adventurous squirrel fell in love with such a lazy spider. Suddenly, the thought quickly changed from Theodore's mind. It was his birthday!

Andrew Anish (9)
Queen Boudica Primary School, Colchester

The Adventure Of Superbunns

One rainy day, Superbunns was going to Planet Minot because he planned to replace the Cyclop's trophy that Professor Cyclop had stolen from the museum with a fake one. He started his jet and zoomed off to Planet Minot. "Boo!" cried Superbunns, scaring his enemy. He dug his fangs into the Professor's skin. He hit the professor, using the hilt of his sword, and snatched the Cylop trophy, replacing it with the replica. He entered his jet and returned to Planet Bunns to place the trophy back in the museum. Afterwards, he drove to the stadium where he was hailed a hero.

Sharen Gnanavel (8)
Queen Boudica Primary School, Colchester

Demon

The Demon had nine tentacles and nine eyes. He lived on Planet Mars and regularly travelled to other planets. He was only nine years old and hadn't yet identified any skills or talents.
One day, he met his friend, Dave, who he hoped would help teach him some skills. Luckily, Dave had a machine that could teach you any skill you wished for. Demon entered the huge machine multiple times. Now he was full of talents and skills.

Umar Tufail (9)

Queen Boudica Primary School, Colchester

The Vamevilielan Who Has The Biggest Secret!

One day, a little monster came out of her lair and she indeed had a worry. *It was her first day of school!* But it wasn't a monster school, it was a *human* school and Vamevilielan didn't know she was a monster.

Inside, she felt like she was going to explode. She packed her bag and set off, hoping nobody would notice. But then, she realised she had forgotten the biggest worry of all... When she looked at people, she could freeze them.

She got to school and nobody noticed she was a monster. She felt relieved.

At break, the strangest thing happened... Her power went away!

Lyla Taylor (10)
Ralph Sadleir Middle School, Puckeridge

81

Mr Furious Fluff Monster

This is Mr Furious Fluff Monster, he's very furious and causes a lot of mischief and he breaks everything.
He goes to the park and dents the slide. He goes to school and snaps a pencil. He goes to a cinema and chucks popcorn. These are some of the reasons why he's called Mr Furious Fluff Monster. Another reason is that one day he turned from an animal (a cute panda) to an angry, fluffy monster and started raging everywhere he went and couldn't stop, that's how he became Mr Furious Fluff Monster.
The red creature is uncontrollable! That's Mr Furious Fluff Monster.

Freddie Durr (11)
Ralph Sadleir Middle School, Puckeridge

Catastrophe

One day, a scientist tried to clone a cat. But it went seriously wrong, resulting in the cat to be very unmerciful. The scientist called the cat CATastrophe, which was an understatement. The cat scratched up: furniture, toiletries, garden, food, anything it could get its claws on. Every day, the scientist would come home with fresh wounds and those wounds developed into scars that were very noticeable.

One day, his wife said, "Look, I have had *enough!*" The scientist got scared that she was going to leave him...

Beau Tollfree (10)
Ralph Sadleir Middle School, Puckeridge

The Laughing Monster

The Laughing Monster, oh how funny he was. And by the way, he had two brothers named Todd. The only difference was that the two Todds were purple and brown and one had some spots. Anyway, The Laughing Monster every day wondered and pondered. The thing he wondered and pondered about most was why he was the only one head to toe in something gross. And you may be wondering what was so gross, and in fact it was that he always woke up covered in toes! The reason for that, in fact, was because he had seven or eight very pongy feet.

Jodie Smith (11)
Ralph Sadleir Middle School, Puckeridge

The Day Big Ears Took Over

This is the story about the day that the Big Ears took over the crazy planet of heat. Now, you may think this is a good planet, but no. You have to wear a big, heavy suit with a gigantic oxygen tank, and the mask is extremely big so that it goes over ears. Once the shuttle landed, the invasion began. The Big Ears had their ears all flopping around, adding to their weight, but this would help in the future.

But the Big Ears were extremely dumb, so this was a hard fight for the Big Ears, but they still won.

Ostyn Barron (10)
Ralph Sadleir Middle School, Puckeridge

85

The Purple Dog

One morning, I woke up to a loud noise. I went outside to check what it was. The bins were knocked over. I opened a bin and found a purple dog. I decided to bring it inside. It started to lick my hands. Suddenly, they turned purple. I tried to wash them, but I couldn't. When I came back to the room, the dog was gone. I went to bed. When I woke up in the morning, I looked into the mirror and I was all purple. There was a massive hole in the ceiling and a giant purple dog was staring at me...

Levente Radics (10)
Ralph Sadleir Middle School, Puckeridge

What Happened?

Yesterday, my dad came home from work, he said
something crazy happened.
"What happened?" I said.
"It was something extreme, something slimy."
"What happened?" I said.
"It was weird and someone turned to stone."
"What happened?!"
"It was speaking in a weird alien language."
"What happened?!"
"*I saw a monster!*"

Amber York
Ralph Sadleir Middle School, Puckeridge

The Crazy Creatures

There is a crazy thing over there.
And now it is everywhere. Inside, outside, on the stairs.
Everywhere I look, I see one there...

Zoe Barton (10)
Ralph Sadleir Middle School, Puckeridge

Reptiles And Cousins

Reptiles, reptiles, oh so many.
But to name a few...
Alligators snap, lizards clap, frogs jump and snails slump.

Alfie Faber (10)
Ralph Sadleir Middle School, Puckeridge

Whirlwind

Whirlwind was playfully creating tornadoes when (out of the blues of the lake) Tsunami, the great water giant, rose - droplets merging into one monstrous beast. Tsunami threw his mighty axe into one of Whirlwind's legs. He yelled in agony, sending a massive push Tsunami's way, also dragging part of his body with it. Tsunami shrank back momentarily, water vapour escaping from his jaws, and prepared to attack once more. Sensing danger, Whirlwind hurled numerous tornadoes, depriving Tsunami of his limbs. Broken and feeble from Whirlwind's onslaught, Tsunami lazily seeped back into the lake...

Joseph Hall (10)
St Joseph's Catholic Primary School, Langwith Junction

The Dragon

The dragon, who had five eyes and a big mouth, was stinky and scary. He went to the school and wanted to learn with the kids.

In the morning, he came to class very quietly and sat in the chair. When the children came into class and saw the dragon, they were frightened and screamed and shouted. They screamed until the teacher came in and said, "Now what happened?" She was scared but tried to speak with the creature, asking him why he had come there. The dragon explained that he wanted to learn and have a friend. After a conversation, all welcomed him.

Alan Michalik (10)

St Joseph's Catholic Primary School, Langwith Junction

The Scary Monster And Tom

A small eye peered through the window. It was brown and had a smile. He had one dark blue eye and a mysterious nose. His name was Ronnie. "Open this window, Tom!" screamed Ronnie. Tom was Ronnie's owner. Tom had found this creature behind a bush. He wanted a pet, so he thought this was a perfect one and didn't tell anybody. Tom quickly opened the window and welcomed him in. "Let's read a story and sleep," said Tom.

"Sure," replied Ronnie. They read a book and slept and promised that no one would separate them.

Adon Sijo (11)
St Joseph's Catholic Primary School, Langwith Junction

Bluca And Foxiella

One day, Bluca went down to the river Naiomi when Foxiella jumped out of a bush. She started bullying him because his arms and legs were fuzzy. She really scared him. She said, "You look disgusting. Tomorrow, at Monster High School, I'm going to do this again and again and again." Bluca rushed home and told his parents and they told him not to worry and that they would sort it out. The next day, Bluca went to Monster High and Foxiella told him that Mr Felshen told her it wasn't right. She apologised and they were friends again.

Beatrix Fisher (10)
St Joseph's Catholic Primary School, Langwith Junction

The Strange Man

Once, there was a girl called Tia. She had beautiful, long hair. For some reason, she was different to all the other girls, but she didn't know why. One day, she met her friends Molly and Clair. They all walked to school as usual. As they got to school, they saw a strange man at the gates, but usually Mrs Chat was there. They whispered to each other, "Let's pull a prank on him." They thought they would pour a bucket of water on him.

At lunch, they filled up a bucket with water and poured it on him... They never returned.

Elizabeth Batterbee (10)

St Joseph's Catholic Primary School, Langwith Junction

We Hate Books!

Once upon a time, there was a really smart monster who loved reading. This monster was called Zack Wasawsin. No other monster liked books. In fact, everyone hated books. If they saw one, they would destroy it. Zack had to hide his books because if his parents found out, he would get grounded for life. Zack read whenever he could. One day, Zack's parents felt generous and gave him a toy, but they saw him reading and shouted, "*What are you doing?*" Zack tried to explain, but his parents didn't want to hear it.

Bunja Sanno (11)
St Joseph's Catholic Primary School, Langwith Junction

How Am I Not Dead?

Today, I walked past a giant abandoned house. You may think that that's normal, but the house was full of monsters! Let me tell you the story about when Jimmy was eaten!
I (Riley) and Jimmy, my friend, walked by an abandoned house and we saw some creatures in the window, so we went in. In the blink of an eye, the horrific, bloody monster stood, smiling at Jimmy. I did nothing but run away, but when I came back, he was decapitated. This was petrifying, but the thing is, *I* am the monster. Jimmy deserved it...

Maja Wator (10)
St Joseph's Catholic Primary School, Langwith Junction

The Lonely Dragon

Once upon a time, there was a dragon who lived in the forest and had no family or friends.
Later in the day, a little girl called Anna commenced her walk in the forest and she found the dragon alone. At first, she wanted to run away but the dragon said, "Please don't go!" He paused. "I have no one to play with and I haven't got a family." Anna came closer to the dragon. Then, they started playing, singing and laughing together. The dragon was overjoyed because he had someone to play with.

Abibatou Kassama (10)
St Joseph's Catholic Primary School, Langwith Junction

Mythic Land

One sunny day, in a land called the Mythic land, there was a monster called Skelly (its real species is a skeleton) with other species like wizards, unicorns, giants and mermaids. All these species have special and interesting powers to defeat evil. Skelly has the power of flying and invisibility. Then one day, Skelly came across an abandoned mansion where he saw a purple portal that had a wizard beside it. He went near it when the wizard told him to go in. He finally went into the portal, but what will he discover?

Briana Carmody (11)
St Joseph's Catholic Primary School, Langwith Junction

Friends Forever

Once upon a time, there was a creature. It was a dog and it was a fox mixed together. It was called Marley. Marley had a great family. She had a brother, sister, mum and dad. Her sister was called Lacie and her brother was called Merlin. Marley lived on a different type of planet. The planet was called Bibbot. Once she was five years old, she started school and met her friends. They were called Misty, Pickle and Mark. They were friends until Year 5, Misty had to leave. Marley said Misty could live with her.

Aoife Harper (10)
St Joseph's Catholic Primary School, Langwith Junction

The Mighty One

Once upon a time, there was a princess who lived in a tower. This pretty princess was wanted by every man in the kingdom of Fairytale Land, but this fabulous lady was guarded by a ten-foot-tall ogre with five eyes and an extremely hairy chin. This ancient beast would stomp on anybody who would try to save the princess. This beast was being paid by the princess' evil mother, The Queen of the Sea. The big, stinky beast had a wife and three kids. His wife protected the prince until one day...

Lola Gale (10)

St Joseph's Catholic Primary School, Langwith Junction

Verki's Life

Hello, my name is Verki. My job is to stop all of people's illnesses. I have already made a medicine called Monster-Sickness Healer. I have already saved 1 million monsters' lives. I get paid 200,000 monster coins. I like my job because I get to see my friends. We became friends after I saved their lives with my healing medicine. My favourite brother is called Boblokie. He is 209. My car is called a Moneymon Monster Car, I got it for 150 monster coins.

Freddie Marriott (10)
St Joseph's Catholic Primary School, Langwith Junction

101

The Mystery Of The Dobble Gangers

Dive into the mind-boggling mystery of the Dobble Gangers.
Dobble Gangers are legendary creatures who are a facsimile of real people, and if they meet that person, that person will die!

Zitel Onyeneke (10)

St Joseph's Catholic Primary School, Langwith Junction

Ziggy Zog

Ziggy Zog was intrigued. Zog pondered what this strange looming thing was. Zog decided to step through the mysterious thing. He said farewell to his family. "Wow!" said Zog. "That was astonishing! Wait, I can smell loneliness..." Zog sprinted tirelessly to the school playground. Finally, Zog spied a little girl sobbing in the bathroom. "What's bothering you?" he questioned as he sucked the loneliness out of her.

"I couldn't thank you more," the little girl said.

"Can I help you get home?"

"Can you take me home with you?"

"If I can get home, you can!" exclaimed Ziggy Zog. And they both went home, as happy as a clam.

Alice Jamieson (9)
St Paul's Cathedral School, London

Missing Girl

One day, at boarding school, Lavender went to lessons as normal. At lunch, she couldn't find her best friend, Daisy. After twenty minutes, she slouched down on her starchy grey blankets in her room... but then, she saw Daisy's rainbow diary. Should she open it? She decided it was her only chance. When she opened it, she saw pink post-it notes covered, in the word 'monster'. She realised something might have taken her. She jumped up and ran out of the door, through the colourful corridor...

When she got outside, in front of her was this horrifying, purple monster holding Daisy. *I must save her.*

Emmeline Farrow (9)
St Paul's Cathedral School, London

A Tired Day

It was another gloomy day in Antarctica. All the penguins where slouching on their eggs. Suddenly, a fin poked out of the freezing water. It got closer and closer...

"Shark!"

All the penguins started sliding on their plump, soft tummies. Shark threw its body on the icy surface and started viciously snapping its tired jaw. Managing to heave its body back into the sky-blue, miserable water, splashing down to the forgotten sea, soon after the exotic moment, the penguins returned to their waiting home with all the adorable, fluffy hatchlings waiting. *Goodness, what a day it was!* they thought.

Madeleine Hirst (8)
St Paul's Cathedral School, London

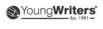

Life On Planet Egg

Once, there was an alien called Mblob. Mblob lived on Planet Egg. Mblob is blue goo with eyes. Planet Egg was dry with little water, Mblob is shy.

One day, Mblob saw something big on fire... Mblob was confused.

"Look!" said Rob.

"I know!" said Dan.

"Look at this species!" exclaimed Rob.

With one look, they took Mblob, so Mblob did what he had to do. Mblob jumped and turned the wheel to Planet Egg. Mblob arrived at Planet Egg.

"Mblob!" shouted everyone.

Mblob and the other aliens lived happily ever after on Planet Egg.

Victoria Elisa Adell Peric (9)
St Paul's Cathedral School, London

London's Problems

The plane skidded to lovely London. When Galen arrived, there was a terrible thunderstorm. London was in ruins all because of a villain named Crystal Claws, Galen thought he had to do something! Galen approached Crystal Claws with courage, luckily he had very bad eyesight. Galen tiptoed up to him and thought: *let's make a plan to destroy him*, so he hid behind a building and thought of a plan. The plan was: to make a catapult and send him into the sea. Once again, Galen tiptoed up to Crystal Claws and silently rolled the catapult up the hill. Galen catapulted Crystal Claws.

Ariana Mangal (8)
St Paul's Cathedral School, London

107

The Big Village Calamity

Once upon a time, there lived a creature called Jeff. He lived in Smart Land, he had blue eyes. A few weeks later, something was haunting the village. People were scared and someone was in danger. Who was this thing and where did it come from? Then, someone screamed, "Someone's been stolen!" There were gasps around the village. Jeff went to investigate and found him in the densest forest in the whole world, then they had a seat on a rock. They went to a village.

"It's the right village!" shouted Jeff. Or is it the right village?

Daniel Snowden (9)
St Paul's Cathedral School, London

The Tale Of Gamboni Swamp

In 1976, a caterpillar-like creature called Cattaspare was drinking some water with the Gnomes who live on his back, just then they heard... *gunshots!* It was the hunters! However, Cattaspare gobbled them up, viciously. But they realised that one Gnome was missing! Happily, a Gnome found a photo of the missing Gnome. Then, a few new hunters came and one of them had a sack with a Gnome inside. But luckily, Cattaspare gobbled them up, again.

So, they had a party and the hunters turned good. While scarily, behind them, the shadow of a man lurked...

Jaxon Reilly Sweeney (9)
St Paul's Cathedral School, London

Z-Blob's Big Adventure

It was a dark, murky night, Z-Blob was fighting the Nightmare King's minions in the Dreamzz Dimension. He turned into a rusty robot, using the magical hourglass, but suddenly, he froze and started to glitch. He used too much power! Then, he unfroze, never feeling so much pain, so he went to the doctors. They said to rest, but he could not stop; his people needed him. Out of nowhere, an unexpected alarm went off at the bank, it was the Nightmare King! Z-Blob was ready to fight. He punched, kicked, but the Nightmare King was too powerful! Z-Blob was done.

Jack Nelson (8)
St Paul's Cathedral School, London

Sam's Adventures

Sam was part hamster and part boy. He was rejected by his beloved family when he was a baby but he still had a necklace with an 'S' on it.

Sam lived in an orphanage where he was teased about the hamster parts of his body. He was frequently bullied, though he didn't care.

One day, someone left the oven on overnight in the orphanage and it set the place on fire. Everyone escaped but Sam's rubbish bin got set on fire and he got burnt. After that, he acquired the power of fire. But the question is, did he survive...?

Francesca Chopin (8)
St Paul's Cathedral School, London

The Great Chase

Zogul is the king's guard.

One day, an evil magician appeared in the king's chamber, killed the king, and disappeared through a time portal. Zogul had to catch this murderer! The time portal was closing, Zogul had to act fast, so he ran through and landed with a crash.

In the distance, he could see the crook. He caught up with him, turned around and saw that he was the king's guard. A fierce battle commenced. Zogul had to defeat him!

Hours later, victorious, he returned to the palace and was crowned king!

Raphael Sen (9)
St Paul's Cathedral School, London

Big Guy

The Big Guy ventured to the magnificent surface of the ocean. Humans spotted him and misunderstood him as a predator. Even though he wanted to be friends, people violently threw rocks at him. He forcefully struck the wall, causing a vicious gust of wind to hit the coast and leaving the humans stunned. However, the Big Guy tried to go back home. Humans were shocked to realise that he was stronger than them and wanted to become allies. They delightedly agreed and humans went up to the ocean's surface while the Big Guy stayed.

Minjun Kim (8)

St Paul's Cathedral School, London

Missing

Upon the highlands, John was brawling with his friend. It was getting cold, so they went inside. Just then, someone or something opened the door and kidnapped his friend. John sprinted to save him but couldn't reach him in time. While John was scurrying across a path he fell into a hole and saw his friend chained up and something grabbed John and chained him up too. Will they escape or not...? A week later, they broke out by using all their strength to break the chains and safely strolled back home... or did they?

Henry Kay (9)
St Paul's Cathedral School, London

Mia's Story

It was just a normal day in Tesco. The shelves were being stacked very high and everything was quiet when suddenly a robber arrived! He loaded his big sack with stuff and *bang!* He pushed everything out of the way as he tried to run away. The shop assistants didn't know what to do.

All of a sudden Mia arrived and she looked like a normal bunny, but actually she was a ninja bunny! She moved with the moves of a starfish and her eyes flashed red. She grabbed the robber's massive sack and saved the day.

Vivienne Roberts
St Paul's Cathedral School, London

115

War Of The Gods

Ra ruled the world. He was the most powerful god. The evil god Set, god of chaos, grew jealous of Ra. Set created an army of demons to build a temple of fire to strengthen his power. One day, Ra found out and led an army of gods to destroy the temple. Ra won and forced Set to fight Apophis, the god of darkness, for all eternity in a prison of doom. The prison was placed in the underworld to be guarded by spirits and even the god of the underworld, Osiris.
After a million years, Apophis defeated Set.

Gustas Ciapas

St Paul's Cathedral School, London

The No-Longer-Lonely Horse

Once upon a time, there lived a lonely horse, his name was Coygy. He lived an easy life, but he had no family, though he had ten friends.
One day, he felt lonely again. He started to cry and hid under his bed. He was really sad. This particular day, he met one of his friends in the park. One said something surprising, "Can I marry you?"
He said, "Yes!"
They had a big wedding, they invited all of their friends, they had a big wedding cake. And they lived happily ever after.

Noah Middleton Targett (8)
St Paul's Cathedral School, London

The Monster's Dream

In the deep dark woods, Wazzle had an amazing walk. Wazzle went through twists and turns. Up she ran on the perfect path of wishes. The glistening sun was shining in the bright sky. Wazzle stared at the cotton candy clouds, thinking of a dream. The dream swayed like the whistling wind. Opening her eyes, she saw a door. She scampered through the golden door, not thinking what she was doing. *Slam!* The door shut. Wazzle was trapped in complete darkness. She wished to go home. *Poof!* She was.

Lyra Evers (8)
St Paul's Cathedral School, London

Mr 1,000,000

A monster named Mr 1,000,000 was stranded in a dry, boiling desert. He tried everything but just couldn't get out.
One day, Mr 1,000,000 saw something moving in the bushes... then, out popped a terrifying creature! He ran to the nearest hiding place frantically! He hid there for hours on end. Until he thought the beast was gone, but he wasn't! He was still there, but Mr 1,000,000 noticed someone else fighting the horrific creature. It was an armed fighter who had somehow found the monster!

Benjamin Lester (8)
St Paul's Cathedral School, London

Barnaby And The Bullies

One day, there was a boy called Barnaby, He was one of the kindest creatures in the world. But the thing was, he was very unusual. He had travelled up to the surface for the first time ever and realised there was a cave on top of a hill. He decided to check it out. When he got up there, it seemed there were beings of his kind. But there was also a Gigabig, a cute pig that was bullying his kind. Barnaby jumped in, scared the pig that was bullying his new friends, and lived happily with them forever.

Oscar Lampo (9)
St Paul's Cathedral School, London

Bobolu And The Microscopic Ant

Bobolu, half bear, half horse, trotted along the Venus-hot Arozona desert. Suddenly, he bumped into a microscopic and suspicious *ant!*
"*Aaaaaaaaaaaaaaaaah!* An ant!" Bobolu shouted.
"Bro, relax, I am an ant, how can I hurt you?" he calmly said. Then, Bobolu trotted along the Venus-hot Arozona desert.
As soon as he got to the other side, courageous hordes of ants came pinning him down. He thought they were nice, apparently not...

Elsa Hildreth (8)
St Paul's Cathedral School, London

The Snug 2000

As you can see, there was a boy called Eric. He was playing a video game until a crash on Eric's window.

It was a cat. "I had no idea who it was," said the boy.

It was Snug 2000 and the boy said, "*No, stop it!*" He shouted, he was extremely frustrated.

Snug 2000 was so bad that he threw him out the sharp window.

Oliver Dudley (8)
St Paul's Cathedral School, London

A Life Of ADHD

It was my first day at school and no one had any special needs but me, I had ADHD. ADHD makes you hyper, very angry. I got angry so much that they kicked me out of school.

One year later, I got into a special school but full of monsters! I was bullied by lots of monsters but then a monster terrified the bullies away, then he asked me, "Do you want to be my friend?"

I said yes please, then I asked, "Do you have ADHD?"

He said, "Yes, I do." Then, more monsters were told about ADHD. ADHD is important!

Ilyas Ali (9)
The Ridge Academy, Cheltenham

The Devouring Demon

One dark and frosty night, Johnny woke up with a chill and heard the shattering of glass. He went down to see what happened and was shocked to see, standing there in the dark, was a Demon. Johnny screamed in terror and ran to his parents' room, but they were gone! He ran to his sister's room and she had vanished. Freaked out, Johnny tried to call the police, but there was no signal. He remembered about the secret room in the house. He ran as fast as his little legs could handle. Johnny was never seen again...

Leland Hannis (10)
The Ridge Academy, Cheltenham

The Funniest Joke In The World!

Once upon a time, there was a man called Bob. He was the funniest man in the world, but one day no one laughed when he told a joke. He told another and the same thing happened. He told another and another and no one laughed. So, he set off to try and find the funniest joke in the world...
A week passed, he had already looked all around his block but couldn't find it. Just as he was going to give up, he found the funniest joke in the world. Everyone at school was laughing.

Henry Holden (9)
The Ridge Academy, Cheltenham

Gast And Me

Under my bed, there was a crazy creature called Gast. He went to school with me in my taxi. At school, he copied the teacher. He taught all the lessons. Gast likes to sing lots of songs, and he sings to all the children. The children danced when they heard him. They really liked his songs.
At the end of the day, Gast came home with me and ate cod fish fingers. He only ate cod! We played together and then I made a bed for him in my treehouse.
Goodnight, Gast.

Dominic Davis (7)
The Ridge Academy, Cheltenham

Charlie's Nightmare

Once upon a time, a ten-year-old boy named Charlie Potter was sleeping and he was awakened by stomping footsteps. He opened the door and what he saw next shocked him to his deep, dark core. Standing in front of Charlie was a tall animatronic with big, sharp teeth and it was black. A very scary person (Nightmare) trapped him and he turned into Nightmare and he wasn't seen forever.
Where could Charlie be?

Charlie Bennett (10)
The Ridge Academy, Cheltenham

Slimy

The Slimy Monster goes inside people's brains and gives them nightmares. One day, the Slimy Monster went inside Lenny's brain while he was asleep. Then, he got a nightmare that a monster was after him. Lenny escaped and SpongeBob was the monster. He tried to make him into a Krabby Patty and put lettuce in Lenny's mouth. Lenny woke up scared but realised he was safe in bed.

Lenny Aves (9)
The Ridge Academy, Cheltenham

The Helpful Creature

There once was a creature called Tore. I found him at the park in a sand pit. Tore was a friendly creature who helped children at the park be safe. One day, a little boy was about to fall off a slide. Tore quickly stuck out his tentacles to save him. The boy said thanks and from then on, Tore always helped children and parents.

Wyatt Campbell (7)
The Ridge Academy, Cheltenham

129

Monsterland

One day, there was a monster called Creepy Crawly. He had seven googly eyes and green skin. He had no friends and was lonely. Creepy Crawly was walking in the park when he saw another monster. Creepy Crawly made him his friend and he wasn't lonely now.
Happily ever after.

Riley Parker (8)
The Ridge Academy, Cheltenham

Creepy Creatures

One day, The Blood Stain of Death is flying over the hot place. He crash-lands in an acid lake and is happy. He spots Creepy Crawly, another monster, and fights him. He shoots blood and acid into Creepy Crawly's eyes until he dies.
The Blood Stain of Death celebrates.

Archie Vaughan (8)
The Ridge Academy, Cheltenham

131

The Monster Under The Bed

The monster was down the stairs, making cookies, so the boy heard banging. He just went back to sleep.
The next morning, it was in his wardrobe. He checked and then his mum checked, it was not there so his mum said, "Did you get enough sleep?"

Micah Dewberry (9)
The Ridge Academy, Cheltenham

Blood Soul

Once upon a time, on a dark night, Blood Soul drank people's blood in the dark.
Then, when he saw Bat Monster, they battled with blood. Then, Bat Monster got smacked on the head and Blood Soul won.
Happy ever after.

Junior (8)
The Ridge Academy, Cheltenham

Living With Autism

I was in my room and I saw a silhouette of a hairy monster that was big and shy.
So, I waited for it to calm down and it was actually really nice, and I never told anyone else.
I brushed his hair and I made his hair.

Rowan Winterford (9)
The Ridge Academy, Cheltenham

Izzie The Invisible Monster

Every day at Monster School, Izzie put up her invisible hand to answer the teacher's questions. She never ever got picked. Izzie became angry until one day, she shouted, "*Let me answer!*" The class were terrified.

"Who said that?" said Mrs Scare.

"I wish you could all see me," sobbed Izzie. That night, walking home, a wizard appeared.

"Drink this magic potion and your wish will come true!" he said with a smile.

Izzie gratefully drank the potion.

The next day, to Izzie's amazement, she heard, "Hello, my name is Freddie Fang.

He can see me?! "Hello, I'm Izzie and I can't wait to be friends!"

Maisie Portas (8)
Wynyard CE Primary School, Wynyard

A Day In The Life Of Jeremiah The Slug

Long ago, a creature named Gruggle was playing with his best friends, Shmunguss, Jeffrey and Jeremiah. Suddenly, they heard raucous footsteps advancing towards them. Foolishly, they pondered whether they were safe at the gloomiest depths of the jungle. They turned and sprinted faster than a dash of lightning.

Gruggle boomed resentfully, "It's your fault, Jeffrey!" Gruggle stormed over to a tree and swiftly chained himself to it. Immediately, a colossal human plucked him off the ground and strutted away. Sluggishly, Jeremiah led Shmunguss and Jeffrey to courageously save Gruggle. Abruptly, the human gave way and everything was natural.

Hazel Swinney (8)
Wynyard CE Primary School, Wynyard

The Best Day Of My Whole Entire Life!

Like others, Bingle was bored. Once the bell rang, he dashed over to the playground, he played with his best friends, Mike and Jackie. Suddenly, his enemies, Phoebie and Ella, came over to him and laughed at him. It happened every day until he finally stood up for himself. He said, "Don't laugh at me, or else!"

Phoebe, the foolish leader, intimidated him by saying, "Or else what?"

With a fierce, angry face, Bingle, ignoring them, said, "I'll tell you off."

She said, "Okay, then."

A teacher then helped them be friends. From then on, they began to get along together.

Anna McCaul (8)
Wynyard CE Primary School, Wynyard

Enemies To Friends

Firefrog played, but he didn't notice that Slimy Spider was lurking behind the trees. Until he heard a sound and then saw slime. He had only once seen slime and then he realised: it must've been Slimy Spider.

"*Hey, you stole my home,*" replied Slimy Spider. Firefrog was confused but then remembered he recognised the slime from when his parents stole the house from the spider. Immediately, Firefrog apologised and then he thought of an idea...

"Why don't you come live with me?" he asked.

The spider thanked him and they both happily walked home and played together.

Harjan Toor (8)
Wynyard CE Primary School, Wynyard

Moltolovagog's Wish

Moltolovagog lived in Tinkotown with the universe's cutest creature (Gigygooga). Moltolovagog was the second-cutest creature in the universe.

He wished upon a shooting star to be the cutest, but didn't realise it was shooting backwards. Over the following days, he got less and less cute until he was simply terrifying.

He travelled to the Gods and found out he wished to the backwards God and he was granted an opposite wish. The nicest God, Lingsa, tried to change him back, but could only get Moltolovagog to 5th-cutest, but he was happy because his friend got to be the second-cutest.

Naia Sedley (9)
Wynyard CE Primary School, Wynyard

The Mini Monsters Help Again

Far away, on the mini-monster planet Zunzagi, a strange, blue fox was creeping around, inspecting trees. He took an axe and chopped one down. This was no ordinary tree, it was a sloth home and these homes were being destroyed. The mini-monsters followed the fox that led them to a clearing full of sloth homes. Wanting to protect the sloths, the mini-monsters jumped out and shouted, "Stop, you naughty fox!"

Realising his mistake, the fox said, "I am sorry I was making a den." The fox vowed to stop. Another Zunzagi habitat saved by the mini-monsters!

Arabelle Waller (8)
Wynyard CE Primary School, Wynyard

The Eruption

One day, Qwerty, a beautiful, magical monster, woke with a loud *bang!* Suddenly, the ground started to shake, Qwerty was brave enough to erupt out of the underworld. The children saw Qwerty and ran straight towards him then he held out his strong hand and... they froze, he looked around, then he hid and clapped. Suddenly, Qwerty unfroze the children. They were confused and he never, ever returned to the outer world, all they know is that he is scared of the big, scary galaxy. But who knows what's out there really in the world, maybe even the galaxy?

Jaxon Dea (8)
Wynyard CE Primary School, Wynyard

141

Speedy Swift And The Difficult Away Game

Speedy Swift the alien had started at a new school. He looked different to humans, so people weren't always kind to him. He had three eyes and three legs.

One day, the school held trials for their football team. He used his extra leg to score amazing goals, better than the coaches have ever seen. He used his extra eye to scan behind him so that he knew where the defenders were so he never got tackled.

The team were so excited for their first match with their new star player. Everyone wanted to be his friend. They realised differences can be good.

Miles Heward (9)
Wynyard CE Primary School, Wynyard

Valuable Lessons

I am Icup. The year is 2121. A year ago today, I killed 5% of the population! Immediately, the government agents found me and dispatched me to Mars in their invisible spaceship.

Life on Mars has been a journey discovering my kind of people. The last year taught me to appreciate life by seeing others in poverty, who work as a community to grow crops and become independent.

I became regretful and sorrowful for what I did. Instantly, I was transported back to Earth. My mission now is to make sure people like me do *not* make the same mistake...

Rishabh Mitra (8)
Wynyard CE Primary School, Wynyard

The Crazy Creature Of Iceland

One day, a young brown-haired girl took a wander through Iceland. As the stars shone, she came across a peculiar animal running across the landscape. It was a small, hairy creature that was somehow brave enough to edge closer. The girl wondered what animal this creature could be. Was she dreaming? It became clear that this was not a dream.

At her feet, there was a small creature looking at her innocently. She figured it was in need of help. The girl picked up the creature and took it back to the lodge so it had a place to stay that night.

Amelia Robertson (9)
Wynyard CE Primary School, Wynyard

The Lonely Monster

Meet Kevin the Kraklops; this species is a cross between a Kraken and a Cyclops. Kevin lived in a ravine, all alone because he looked scary due to his fangs and his bulging, unblinking eye. He hated living alone. Months went by and he got lonelier and lonelier.

One day, he saw a fish trapped in the rocks. He knew if he saved the fish people would trust him, so he moved the rock and freed the fish. The fish told his friends what he'd experienced and soon Kevin was being recognised. Kevin made friends and never felt lonely again.

Alexander O'Rourke (9)
Wynyard CE Primary School, Wynyard

Fight Back

Once upon a time, in a little town, a young girl was in her small home when the sky darkened. Out of the corner of her eye, she saw it! Eyes glowed green, skin as dark as ash and its mouth shone brighter than the sun. After the flames calmed down, there was nothing but ash.

She swore she would fight back.

Many years passed as she trained and trained until she was ready. She climbed up the mountain until she found the beast. She fought for one week.

She had done it!

She looked up to see... another dragon!

Matthew Brown (9)
Wynyard CE Primary School, Wynyard

The Wish Monster

On a faraway island lives the wish monster, who hears wishes from little children and tries his best to make them come true. He was very happy with his job but was also, very lonely.

Suddenly, he heard a wish from a little girl called Sophia. Sophia was like him because all she wanted to do was to make everyone happy. The wish monster was afraid Sophia would be scared of him because he was different. He was brave and magically appeared in front of Sophia. She cried tears of joy and thanked him for making her wish come true.

Poppy Lightowler (9)
Wynyard CE Primary School, Wynyard

A Lant's Life

Once upon a time, there was a little Lant. You might be wondering what a Lant is. A Lant is a lion mixed with an ant and it lives in a tropical rainforest. He goes for an adventurous walk in the forest!

On Lant's long walk, he passes under gigantic trees and gets tired, so he stops to rest and goes to sleep. He wakes up with a *bang!* Lant opens his eyes and sees a huge green leaf trapping him...

Lant roars loudly, the leaf comes off. Lant turns left and is faced with a chameleon!

Tea is served!

Toby Guyatt (9)
Wynyard CE Primary School, Wynyard

The Luraf Is Under My Bed!

Help! There is a Luraf under my bed! What is it? Is it dangerous? Is it mean? I'm too scared to go to bed, it might eat me! I don't know what it looks like, but I know it's there. I have to be brave, I have to be strong, so I'm going to look!
When I look under my bed, I see an evil monster with razor-sharp teeth, bright red eyes and fifteen legs!
It chases me down the hallway, out of the house and down the street, but then it starts crying, it just wanted to be friends.

Luca Caruana (9)
Wynyard CE Primary School, Wynyard

Five-Eyed Naughty Aliens

Hello, my name is Smarty Party and I have ten skills and ten tricks. I have five alien friends called Jack, Ben, Jaxon, Max and Lucas. I also have five dragon enemies called Harjan, Felix, Archie, George and Bobby. They all got into a fight, Harjan, Felix and Archie died from the dragons, Jaxon and Jack died from the aliens.
Everyone was sad that their friends had died, so everyone started playing together and became friends.

Ben Maudlin (8)
Wynyard CE Primary School, Wynyard

YOUNG WRITERS INFORMATION

We hope you have enjoyed reading this book – and that you will continue to in the coming years.

If you're a young writer who enjoys reading and creative writing, or the parent of an enthusiastic poet or story writer, do visit our website **www.youngwriters.co.uk**. Here you will find free competitions, workshops and games, as well as recommended reads, a poetry glossary and our blog.

If you would like to order further copies of this book, or any of our other titles, then please give us a call or visit **www.youngwriters.co.uk**.

Young Writers
Remus House
Coltsfoot Drive
Peterborough
PE2 9BF
(01733) 890066
info@youngwriters.co.uk

Scan me to watch the Crazy Creatures video!

f YoungWritersUK   **𝕏** YoungWritersCW

⊙ youngwriterscw   **♪** youngwriterscw